The Stories They Told Me

The Stories
They Told Me

Melissa Gillman

To order additional copies of this book, contact:
Xlibris Corporation
1-888-795-4274
www.Xlibris.com
Orders@Xlibris.com
44028

CONTENTS

This book is dedicated to all the people who shared parts of their lives with me.

These individuals told me their stories openly and voluntarily and none were divulged "in confidence". Even so, all the names have been changed as have various other details in order to protect the privacy of each individual. Accordingly, this book is a work of fiction.

This book was only possible through the continued support and patience of my husband Barry, without whom I could not have come this far.

Author's Note
Regarding Proceeds from this Book

All my royalties from this book will go to "Madison's Caring for Kids with Cancer".

Madison Honig is a teenager living in Florida, now recovering from Hodgkin's Lymphoma after battling through chemotherapy for an extended period. Why did I pick this particular charity? That's a story that deserves a place in a book of stories like this one.

I met Madison's mom, Leslie, when we were both ten years old, and we were best friends as we grew up in New York City during the sixties and seventies. As we got into careers, marriage and children, we exchanged calls and letters, but somewhere along the way we both must have moved house once too often, and we lost touch with each other about twenty years ago.

I kept searching sporadically: after all the "internet can do anything", but to no avail. Then a few months ago, I was checking an old voice-mail account. We no longer used it actively, but I'd check it every six months or so. There was a message from Leslie, date stamped four months previously, so long that she'd given up hope of getting a return call. REUNION!!!

But Leslie was in Florida, I was in California, and there seemed to be no early date when we'd get together. As we were catching up by phone and email on twenty "missing years", she told me about the challenges the youngest of her four children, Madison, had endured in beating cancer. Not only had Madison persevered through her own chemo treatments, but she had decided to raise money to make life a bit easier for other children suffering from cancer.

A local TV show had publicized Madison's story and in the TV clip, mentioned she and her family had been awarded a week's vacation in Hawaii and announced the dates and location. I couldn't believe my eyes: it was the same week and location that we had booked almost a year previously. So we finally had our reunion, and I got to meet my old friend and her family, including the bright and determined Madison, then seventeen years old.

So that's the story of why the royalty proceeds are going to this charity. To explain how the funds are used, I'll turn to Madison's own words:

> *While going through treatment for my Hodgkin's Lymphoma last year, I realized how many young kids are affected with cancer. The process for treating cancer is by no means easy. This is especially true when you have to spend numerous hours a day on an examination table while getting outpatient chemotherapy. As I watched parents trying to comfort their children, which seemed sometimes impossible, I wondered if there was anything I could do. Now being in remission, I am passionate about providing comfort for the young heroes at All Children's Hematology-Oncology Clinic.*
>
> *The doctors, nurses, and staff were absolutely unbelievable and extremely gracious. I feel like they are all a part of my family. However, there is a severe lack of comfortable furniture and entertainment for the children. The waiting room is sparse with toys making the days seem even longer for the children and their families. The infusion rooms, which are constantly used, are in dire need of new recliners. The existing chairs are worn and are no longer sufficient for parents to sit in with their children.*
>
> *The goal of this benefit is to provide the treatment center with new recliners and entertainment such as televisions, DVD players, and toys. Recently I was awarded the 2007 Anne Frank Humanitarian Award for my proposal for providing comfort for kids with cancer. I would be honored if you would join me in helping to realize this dream by providing as much comfort as possible for the current and future children undergoing exhausting treatments for their cancer.*

THANK YOU VERY MUCH and I hope you will join me to make all these dreams come true!—Madison Honig

If any reader wishes to donate any additional amount, then please feel free to send a tax-deductible contribution to:

All Children's Hospital Foundation
PO BOX 3142
St. Petersburg, Florida 33731

Please write on the memo line of your check that *"Funds are being donated in honor of Madison Honig and are designated for Madison's Caring for Kids with Cancer account."*

1

Introduction: Starting Out

Growing up, everyone dreams of what they can become. For those of us in show-business, this usually starts at an early age, but eventually the dreams meet up with the realities of life. Many of our ambitions are derailed by the actions or words of others; sometimes our own commitment wavers. This book is a journal of the dreams and the eventual realities of a number of people who shared their stories with me over the course of a year.

Sometimes I wondered why total strangers would sit down next to me and pour out these amazing stories. Maybe it's because many of them were much younger than me and as they thought of me as "ancient", they hoped I'd be able to sympathize without judging them too harshly. These stories are not about me, but you do need to know a bit of my story to understand my perspective on their dreams and the realities of "showbiz life".

My first ballet shoes were fitted when I was four, a half century ago. That was the start of my involvement with stage and screen: a girl from the Bronx, aiming for a career as a dancer. I was hooked from that point on, and I've been involved with the arts ever since. My ballet and dance career lasted only till I was seventeen. At that age, the high point was being selected for the cover of the Danskin brochure. What I didn't realize at the time was the significance of winning a job based on how I looked in dance clothes, not on how I actually danced.

Shortly after that, working with a famous but brutally honest choreographer, I was told that my future in the arts would be better focused on acting, not dance. My dream didn't die, it just evolved (but even now I still take a ninety minute ballet class twice a week). After college, I was accepted into a very prestigious acting class, and managed to stay for many years without ever being "asked to leave". That phrase was their polite translation for "get out; you have no talent". I believed I was on my way to stardom. Little did I know.

I worked in "showcases" all over New York. That involved working unbelievably hard without pay, in hopes that an agent or casting director would "discover you". This turned out to be the total opposite of the showbiz "glamour" image. For example, one New York winter, I was in a show in a theater so small that when you exited stage left, you had to stand out in the cold on the fire escape until your next entrance.

Over the years, I built my career wherever I found work: commercials, print, summer stock, comedy clubs, bit parts in movies, small roles in soap operas, even developing my expertise as a hand model. In my first commercial I played a high school senior. In my most recent, I played a chronic arthritis sufferer. Along the way I moved from commercials for Pampers, up the age range to ads for Depends. It's been a varied and interesting journey.

I never did get "discovered". On the other hand, at various times I've been fired, replaced, intimidated, and generally pushed around, but I kept going. Serious actors don't give up. I've been working for over thirty years, and still enjoy the "business". It helped that I have had a realistic perspective on what to expect from my work, both good and not so good.

It also helped that I built a life away from the camera and stage. Happily married for over twenty-five years, with three grown sons, my work has been an important part of my life, but not my sole focus.

For the past four years I've been living in Southern California after we moved from the New York area for my husband's job. In that context, I was a "fresh face", although an older one than most. For the last year, I found myself involved in a new TV show, working both behind and in front of the cameras. Sounds glamorous, but the real world was different. The show was low budget and high pressure, with scripts rewritten daily. I worked five days a week, and sometimes six, mostly twelve to fifteen hours a day.

On this show, I started out as an extra: "background" or "atmosphere". The name said it all. With up to fifty extras milling around every day, it was pretty clear they needed better management of the "crowd". After a month, I was asked to take over as the "wrangler". Yes, we were out west, but on set this type of wrangler was in charge of the extras. I'd keep our extras organized and (hopefully) alert and ready to go on set, as well as coordinating their movements to and from the crowd scenes, while making sure that all their paperwork was correct before they went home (and that was a job in itself).

The set itself was a crowd scene. On any given day there might have been over a hundred people on the set. As well as the stars, we had the director, the first assistant director, the second assistant director, and the second, second assistant director. There were producers, writers, actors and actresses (daily role players plus those with small parts), wardrobe plus two assistants, hair stylists, a make-up specialist, electricians, cable handlers, general assistants, caterers, food servers: the list went on and on. And at the bottom of the list in the pecking order, there were the extras.

Extras are mostly aspiring actors, and most actors love to talk about themselves. For the as-yet-undiscovered, that's usually because nobody else is talking about them yet. I'm unusual in that I like to listen, not talk. I've also reached the point where I don't have unrealistic aspirations any more, so I was happy to sit and listen. None of these stories were told to me in confidence; the conversations just flowed. I have not written anything that anyone wanted kept private: I do have a very high respect for people's privacy.

For the actors and extras, there was usually a lot of down time during the work day, just waiting to be called on set. For most of that time, the extras were just sitting around waiting and talking among themselves. As well as their ambitions in show business, most were basically trying to sort out their lives off the set, just as we all are. These were not the stars, just the regular men and women trying to get by, or to get their "big break". Their perseverance and strength amazed me. These are some of the extraordinary stories they told me.

2

Helena

As I sat in a comfortable seat in my cop uniform, Helena pulled up a chair next to me. We were working in a police station episode and that day I was one of the extras. I had seen Helena quite often over the previous six months. When she was dressed up she was attractive, but she had very sad eyes and there was clearly an underlying unhappiness. Usually people poured out their story to me only when I was the wrangler, and in charge of the group. That day I was an extra reading a magazine, but that didn't stop her.

Helena was born in Texas forty-one years ago. Life had been very difficult for her, and you could see it had taken a huge toll. Her father left when she was a child, so she grew up with her mother, brother and an abusive stepfather. I was glad that she just left it at that, as I really did not want to know any more details. She grew up as a wild child with a very strict mother and an unavailable step-dad. Her brother dropped out before he could make it through high school. She did make it, but only just. At eighteen her mother and stepfather kicked her out of the house as they couldn't handle her rebellious attitude. After that she stayed with a good friend for three months and managed to finish high school. She shared the same birthday with her mother and when she was thrown out, her mother told her she was glad to see her go so that now she could have her own cake and not have to share it.

After a series of very bad relationships, she got married at twenty-two and had a daughter soon after. Her husband turned out to be horrible: gambling, drinking and also abusive. Unfortunately, sometimes people go to what they know. Even so, she stayed with him for quite some time, afraid to leave, afraid to stay. They got divorced after two and a half years. He's had no contact with his daughter or with Helena over the years, but recently she was tipped off by a friend and found out a lot about him on My Space. He currently had a house in Florida, and ran a number of dubious-sounding businesses. He cleaned her out in the divorce and now he seemed to be enjoying himself. She had neither the funds nor the stamina to go after him. She eventually used those to go after her second husband!

After the divorce she went to Vegas and became a dancer. She had her boobs done and looked great. Then she realized that she could probably make more money as a stripper and she followed that road. She had no money, and with a daughter to support she knew she could at least make a living this way.

Helena worked for many years in Vegas and she said most of the clubs were okay, although a few were really seedy. However she said she was able to keep her morals intact. She bought a townhouse in Vegas and that felt very good, finally to own something. Her daughter was having a difficult time. It was hard for me to imagine the daughter's life. Five years ago, at thirteen, she was diagnosed with a learning disorder, and had to go to a special school. Helena had always said she worried that she couldn't spend more time with her, but she did what she needed to do, including marrying again.

This time it lasted for just two months. This husband had no job but lied that he was in the military. In fact he lied to her about most things in his life. It turned out that he wanted to get his hands on her house, either by having Helena committed or by killing her. He intended to poison her and drugged her little by little. Helena became a physical wreck during the time he was trying to kill her. He inserted an IV in her arm, claiming that he was a medic and that this would help calm her down. In reality it contained a slow acting poison that was very difficult to diagnose. Her daughter saw what was happening and called an ambulance. Helena spent three days in the hospital in intensive care. While she was there, her husband somehow got hold of the papers for the house and transferred the deed to his name. He was able to sell the house and vanished a week later. He had sucked the life out of her.

By that time, Helena was in no shape to take care of her daughter. She sent her to stay with her brother for a while. He lived back in Texas near her mother, but he too was not talking to their mom. Her mother got divorced from Helena's step-father after thirty-three years and now lived alone, working the nightshift at a local factory. Helena's brother also had two divorces behind him and a child from each of his wives. He and the children were living on public assistance. Both his ex-wives were from Mexico and now with their citizenship, they were free to look for better opportunities. He turned out to be a drunk and the house he lived in was filthy, so Helena's daughter came home after two weeks. At this point, Helena had no money, two ex-husbands (one of whom had tried to kill her), no house, no possessions and hadn't spoken to her mother in twelve years.

We were called to do our scene in the police station. She was playing a hooker which she explained to me repeatedly was not the same as a stripper. Helena moved from Vegas to have a better life. It has been a struggle. In reality, she wasn't able to do more than get extra work and an occasional very small role. However, who knows, anything could happen. I knew that she was really broke and would have loved to meet a "normal man": much harder than it sounded. Her daughter was really having problems. How could she not be, given the environment in which she grew up?

Helena was struggling with so many legal hassles. As well as the legal fallout from her marriage, she was trying to get back the money from her inheritance that her grandmother left her. Evidently her cousins took all the money from her grandmother when she was alive. There were substantial amounts invested in houses and other possessions. Helena wound up getting $3,000 which basically paid for her lawyers.

She was getting ready to go home. Her daughter hadn't gone to school that day. She was a senior in high school. When they called a wrap, we packed up our things and headed out. She told me she was going to stop at a wine bar on the way home. Her daughter would continue waiting for her mother. Helena would continue to wait for her life to turn around. She has convinced herself that this was the year for that to happen.

3

Walkie-Talkie

Walkie-talkies are used extensively on any film or TV set. They are the main way for all the supervisors to keep in constant contact with each other, because the sets sometimes are very large, maybe a mile from end to end. When I first had to use one in my role as a wrangler, I was nervous because I was not exactly a "hi-tech" person. It took me a while to learn the Walkie-talkie, and I was always a great source of entertainment as I struggled with the controls and buttons. For some reason, other users thought this was very funny. I hated using my Walkie-talkie because people were constantly talking to you, at you, around you, or even about you. It was in your ear for up to fifteen hours straight and you'd hear conversations from all over.

As I fumbled around the channels, I eventually got much better, but hearing all of that yelling and gossip was just exhausting. I learned that you had to be on the Walkie-talkie all day, and if anyone on our set was heard "keying", which meant making a wrong channel choice, all eyes went to me as they'd learned from experience that I was the most likely culprit. I didn't mind this after a while and I had explained to the assistant director that technology was not my thing. He rolled his eyes and commented "obviously". I told them to take up a collection to get me Walkie-talkie lessons but of course, this never happened. They would put up with my failures on these dumb little machines because I knew how to do my job well.

When you really heard yelling over the Walkie-talkie channels was after someone had made a costly mistake. One time I sent a whole jury pool home before the trial was over. Oops. Fortunately the director was able to shoot the scene from another direction without the jury being on camera. Otherwise it would have cost them a lot of money, and we all knew the bottom line was the dollar bill. I was able to save my job because the director was understanding and intervened, to the chagrin of others who wanted my job.

Some of the things I heard over these channels were very rude, but I must say most of it was really funny. Normally we all started on the same channel but when someone intended to say something extremely bad about someone else, they told their intended listener to switch to another channel. Since everyone else had heard them saying, "Switch to another channel," you could just follow along with them (I learned that much technology, at least).

The one time I found it really not funny was when I heard the wardrobe person and a production assistant call me a retard and a moron. This was on a production unit that had a reputation for insulting everyone, but I wasn't going to take this. I complained to the so-called supervisor: the second-second assistant director. Now there was always a hierarchy of power: typically our director, our first assistant director, our second assistant director and the "second-second", who was often about eighteen years old and didn't really have any power at all. He was shocked (yeah, right) and very apologetic, but wasn't going to do anything.

By the time I finished my day, I had decided I had been insulted enough. It was time to move to a new unit. The production units were named by color: purple, white, green, etc. It seemed strange but actors are visual, not numbers people. They could remember to go to the "green unit", but you wouldn't tell them they were on "Unit 14" and expect a full turn-out. The units were all very different in working atmosphere and how they treated people, and each one had its own individual "character".

Whether a film, a TV show, or a soap opera, in this business every minute had to be budgeted and tracked, right from the time they said, "We're in," which meant we're starting, and the clock has begun ticking. In practice, if it was an early 7 a.m. start, and we didn't get going on time, there was no chance of completing the day's work within the budgeted time period, which was usually twelve hours. If people were not ready or anything went wrong, they were charged with "wasted time", and every minute of wasted time got recorded in the time sheets. There was a timed call to break for lunch, and then one to get back from lunch. There were call times for the first snack, for break time, or for whatever was needed.

My next problem was that everything was done in military time, on a 24-hour clock. Now my skill there was even worse than my skill with the hated Walkie-talkie. I never figured out how those military times worked and usually I was writing these numbers on time-sheets as I was signing fifty or more people out at about one in the morning. Most of the time the second-second who requested me for this job was very patient with me. I was also very careful to make sure that everyone got the right length of time on their time-sheet, even if I was messing up and couldn't tell the difference between 1810 and 2140. It might have taken me a while, but eventually I got it sorted out. Even so, the first day I had to do all of this, I was working in a trailer and it took me so long that the crew started to drive it away to storage for the night as they thought no-one was left on the shoot or in the trailer.

As each day wore on and people were getting tired, some of the male directors or assistants usually decided they would like a little "eye candy". These were any of the beautiful girls who were selected to sit near the director when the day seemed really stretched out. These spots were easy to fill (after all this was Southern California). While I and most other extras were booked on a daily basis, these girls were often booked by the week. When on a break, they'd usually sit on the set with the director, listening to him talk about himself. It looked like mere flirting, but what did I know? I stayed well clear of any of their "after-school activities". The goal was to help the director get through the day, and believe me, by the time it was a wrap and I was heading home, I forgot all about them. Don't know, don't care; I just wanted to go to sleep.

The first assistant director was there to push things along, and to make sure the director was able to do his job well. He stayed by the director on the set all day, relaying the director's instructions to the rest of us and it would be a problem for everyone if either he or the director wasn't pleased.

Early episodes of this show were already on the air each evening. I didn't watch it because I could never stay awake, and even if I recorded it, I spent most of my days-off sleeping. Everyone had their own ideas about this show, and what they hoped to achieve from it. Virtually all were looking to get something out of the experience. Most of the extras watched this show at home all the time to see if they could see themselves, wondering if this could lead to their big break. The irony was that on the set, they did nothing except talk about themselves and eat as much as they could on the meal breaks. Even so, when they came in each day, they were so excited about what their "part" had been in the episode shown the night before. Didn't they realize that we were extras? None of us had "parts" in this show.

The director wanted to go on to direct a regular network TV show. The first assistant director wanted to be a director and the production assistants also wanted to move up. The wardrobe people wanted to be the designers. The makeup people wanted to be "makeup person to the stars". Basically we all knew what we were doing here: we were making low-budget television shows, but even so, we all had ambitions and agendas. I was the only one who had been in the business long enough to know it was a long climb.

The extras had their own ideas of their worth. They continued to show up, even though many of them were frequently late, but they all felt that they were better actors than the people in the main roles. They might have been doing extra work for just four months but they were sure they were going to move up to stardom. They explained they had even read books on acting, they plunked down lots of money to get photographs (usually by bad photographers) and they constantly boasted about their pictures. They had no credits and not one of them had ever been to an acting school, but this show had been a good source of income for them. Even though I hated to generalize, they were totally unrealistic in their expectations.

All the casting directors seemed to feel the same way about the "background". They had little respect for extras and warned actors against getting categorized in this group. Their concern was that it was easy money and that an actor who worked as an extra wouldn't be taken seriously when auditioning for roles. The extras looked at me as a failed person who never made it out of the "holding pen". Sometimes I would mention to them I'd been an actress for twenty-five years. Since they were typically in their early twenties, this had no meaning for them except to scare them because I was older than their mothers. When I told them I had joined the Screen Actors Guild back in 1974, they looked at me with pity because I was so old and as far as they were aware, seemed to have gone nowhere. Of course, they didn't say any of that since I was the one placing them on the set: they were smarter than that. On the other hand, they gossiped so loudly I heard them anyway.

I had become friendly with some of the extras. They were truly amazed when I could help them sort through some of the basic life issues that they were facing. Many had had no real guidance or advice from parents or friends, and at least I could provide that because I had lived more than twice as long as most of them. They thought I was smart because I could spell the names of the shows we were shooting, which really wasn't that tough. Their average reading material ranged from *People* or *Glamour* magazine to the *Enquirer*. I rarely saw any of them open a book or read anything other than a glossy magazine. Many of them just tuned out on their iPods. Usually ten out of my typical thirty-five or forty fell asleep on each shoot. On one set, the second assistant director made someone leave because he snored so loudly he ruined the take.

As each day wore on, we usually started to run behind schedule by around four in the afternoon. I don't think I'd ever been on a shoot in the last thirty years when we finished ahead of schedule. Why? Because even if we were running ahead, the director would say, "You know what? We paid for this whole day, so let's try something new." Tempers would start to flare, especially by the end of the week. The main actors faded a bit by this time and they were exhausted because the hours that they kept were very rough. Sometimes they'd have to shoot all night, and then would have to be on the set the next morning by eleven and shoot the whole way through another day. It took a toll on the actors, physically and mentally. Sometimes the actors just said they needed a little rest. Sometimes they asked for "something to keep them going". Those requests weren't relayed over the Walkie-talkies! But occasionally a vicious sense of humor crept in. One director complained about his star, "Get the makeup team out here because she looks horrible," and the response came anonymously over the Walkie-talkie, "We've done what we can: shoot her from the back."

The last shot of the day was called the "Martini Shot", which meant after it was over, you could go have a martini and relax. By that time, many on the set were just yelling at each other, or threatening not to come back because the conditions were so bad, but we all showed up the next day anyway. In fact, everyone seemed to be worried that they wouldn't be asked back. There was constant whispering on the set, ugly glances, fingers pointing. They even got nervous watching me: anytime I was talking on the phone, all the extras would be looking at me because they thought I was talking to the casting people, like I had no other life. My job was to handle the extras and all their problems. As long as I did that, I didn't call Casting, and they didn't call me. But if I was on the phone, it certainly did seem to worry the extras!

I'd definitely learned to stand up for myself; it was the only way to maintain some respect (although on this set, the respect usually lasted for about a day). Once I overheard the director yelling at the assistant director about the new stand-in, who was me. He said that I was too old and not pretty enough. I stayed the entire day because I've always behaved professionally, and at the end of the day, I went up to the director and shook his hand to say good-bye. However I couldn't resist telling him that the next time he wanted a person who was "younger and prettier", he could call someone else at six in the morning and ask them to show up at seven.

They were quick to show off their power, but underneath, they knew who helped them keep the shooting running smoothly. So, towards the end of the show's production run, I laughed when I overheard the assistant director talking about firing me because I reminded him of his mother. I didn't worry. He was gone by the end of the day. That was a perfect example of what goes around, comes around.

I was probably one of the few people on this set who had no ambition to rise to power on this TV show. I have been very happy doing what I do and I had learned more about TV production on this show in twelve months than I had in several years in various commercials and acting jobs. As well as learning the details of production, I had learned how to manage a large group of people, some of whom couldn't remember which unit they were on, what day it was, or what scene it was. I have walked away with a lot of knowledge that can be applied somewhere else. As long as I don't need a Walkie-talkie in that job!

4

Roberta

Roberta never introduced herself to me when she was a fellow extra. Her manner to everyone was hostile and complaining from the start. She was booked to play the role of an old woman. She was in her sixties, but the impression she gave was of someone even older. The scene was a funeral, and Roberta was playing a well-dressed elderly mourner. She turned out to be yet another person with a fractured life, just one with even more years under her belt than anyone else on the set that day.

By early afternoon, all the extras were told to take a four hour break while the prior day's scenes were being re-shot because of poor lighting. Roberta pulled up a chair next to me and her story poured out.

She went to a strict Catholic school but got pregnant at sixteen. That was in her senior year and she had to leave school in February to "go live with an aunt", missing her high school graduation. She wound up marrying the boy who was the father of her first daughter. That was in 1956, making her in her late sixties now. Roberta went on to have four more children: another girl, then two boys and finally a third daughter. Even so, it remained a very loveless marriage. She was already bitter about life at that young age, and by the time she was twenty-four, her husband was physically and mentally abusing her.

Her husband did not touch the children, but put them in a mental prison. It was so bad she went back to her mother's house. Her mother was glad to take her in, but didn't have enough room for all of them, so she sold her house and bought a bigger one. The seven of them lived relatively happily, even though financially it remained a struggle. The father of these children had mostly disappeared from the scene, sometimes showing up on odd occasions, but that was the sum of his involvement. In those days the legal system wasn't any help to struggling mothers. Unfortunately Roberta was ahead of her time in that there were no laws to protect her and her children, who were growing up without a father figure.

When her older son was sixteen, he was diagnosed with bone cancer. By this time she had divorced her first husband, re-married and then divorced her second husband. Her son was an athlete, but had to have his leg amputated. She said that almost finished her, but she had to carry on: she was a single parent of four other children who all resented her for giving all of her attention to her sick son.

That son actually went on to live an active life, at least for a while. He married at twenty-five and lived another thirteen years before he died from a different cancer. Roberta liked this daughter-in-law. Her daughter-in-law never remarried and still kept in touch with her.

Her other son went on to be "a bum" (her words), and traveled around the country doing "who knows what". She said that he called her every once in a while, usually about three times a year. Every time he called, he was always looking for money, which she didn't have. She told him to call one of his two married sisters instead. Roberta said they married "very well", but now didn't talk to her. They both have had children. One had a daughter and the other had three sons. Her grandsons didn't talk to her much either, and she claimed they're poisoned by their mother's viciousness.

Her youngest child has been living with her. Susan was now nearing forty and has been diagnosed as a severe manic depressive. Roberta told me that she must have suffered from this all of her life, but she was only diagnosed a year after her son was born. Todd was now fifteen, and had never had a father involved in his life. Roberta got full custody of Todd when he was two, as Susan's behavior was uncontrollable, and neither of her sisters would take the boy. After many years of treatment, Susan was finally doing better as long as she took her meds. Unfortunately, that was rarely. Susan now held down a job at Wal-Mart but most of the time did not even remember that she had a son. Nearing seventy, Roberta was effectively the mother of a fifteen year-old son. No-one else in the family would have anything to do with him except Roberta. It turned out to be a very difficult situation.

After two failed marriages and with five children, Roberta had married a third time when she was thirty. Albert was a rich Jewish doctor who had three grown children of his own. He was not much interested in her children who were now growing up and who eventually moved out. In his mind, this was a good thing. Albert was insistent that Roberta convert to Judaism, which she did. I noticed that her belief in her new religion seemed rather superficial: she was wearing a big cross around her neck and talked about "those people" in a negative tone when discussing her Jewish relatives and acquaintances.

This marriage was stable and she got a taste of a much better life. Her husband made at least $500,000 a year. Well, that's what he told her anyway. In reality it was a lot more. Albert's first wife had received a lot in the settlement, but he still managed very well. He did not want Roberta to work and she was happy not to, even though he constantly reminded her of how lucky she was. A part of the reason they stayed together was that Roberta looked the other way a lot: too much as it turned out. The marriage lasted for twenty-three years but when he died, there was no money left. Over the prior eight years he had been portioning out his $3 million estate to his own children and even to his ex-wife. He owned a lot of real estate, some that Roberta didn't even know about.

After his death, his three children came to get the rest of his stuff: furniture, mementos, and things like that. Roberta would not give it to them. He had left the house to her, not to them. She explained that it may not be a very fancy house, just a modest family home, but it was hers now.

As we sat there waiting for her to do her bit part, she got a couple of calls from her grandson Todd. He was home from school. Her face lit up. She clearly adored him and took delight in having him all to herself. It was nice to see that she could smile, if only for a few seconds.

5

Steve

Steve has been playing a waiter, delivering bread and drinks to the same people at the same table for thirteen hours. I had seen him around the set for the past week. At thirty-one, he was dark, slender and handsome.

We spoke for a few minutes during a break. Steve's dad was from Texas and his mom from Vietnam. He had moved to California from Texas and has been going back and forth between the two for the last six years. Steve never got along with his parents. Before he was born, his father had already been married, had two kids and divorced before he was posted to Vietnam by the army. He was so depressed that he went to Vietnam almost hoping to get killed. Instead he met Steve's mom and eventually married her and brought her and her daughter back to the States. They had two more children, a girl, and then Steve, the youngest, and the only son. His father never heard again from his first wife or his first two children and remained an unfulfilled man.

The last time Steve had been back to Texas was after a terrible breakup with his girlfriend, who had gotten pregnant by another man. It wasn't the pregnancy that wounded him, but the feeling of betrayal which he said was so hard that he felt he couldn't continue the relationship.

Even though Steve was intelligent, he had been labeled "slow" during his childhood and he was in remedial classes until the 11th grade. He knew he had to get out of Texas, as he felt the world had much more to offer him, so he joined the Navy and spent three years trying to figure out his life. He learned a lot of life skills, but he remained confused about what he wanted to do.

He moved to Los Angeles, but partied so much, he had to return to Texas to get himself "cleaned up", both mentally and physically. That happened twice. Each time though, he was so bored in Texas, he came back west. For a while Steve worked in Las Vegas, at various casinos and an adult bookstore.

One casino job involved walking around half naked, dressed in ancient Egyptian costume, bringing coals to fire pits.

There he shared an apartment with a lesbian who had gotten pregnant at a sperm bank. When his roommate had the baby, he couldn't cope and moved back to Texas once more. After another six months, he headed back to California for good. He got his first real job at Home Depot. He worked in the paint department and moved up quickly, being promoted to "paint consultant". He went on to teach painting and design, and that job lasted three years. But Steve's history always seemed to include moving on before too much time elapsed. Once again, he left to pursue other interests.

He went on an open call he found on Craig's List and was hired to work as an extra in a TV show. After getting established as a TV extra, he learned that the studio also had a division that worked with the military in preparing troops for life in Iraq. In this "special operations" set, adjacent to the "regular" TV studios, there was an authentic-looking Iraqi village. The studio constantly was looking for extras to play the roles of insurgents and villagers in order to train soldiers in the situations they might encounter in Iraq. Essentially, this was playing "war games" with real soldiers. Steve loved it, and even though there was a lot of physical action, he has never been hurt. As well as being an exciting job, it has been a great service that he was doing. He had recently joined a special group that went on two week missions to different locations around the country.

Steve was delighted that he had been hired for this show as an extra. He even got a line. At thirty-one, he still had a lot of living to do. Our ten minute break was over. We returned to our places on the set. I wondered what else I would have learned if the break was longer.

6

Ann

We had been shooting a murder scene poolside at the luxury mansion rented as our location for that week. I was huddled in my warm clothes. Ann sat outside with the extras and film crew on a dinner break. She was wearing a tank top with her breasts sticking straight out. The rest of us were in sweatshirts and jackets, as the evening temperature dropped and it was by then barely 50 degrees. She had just come from Wisconsin: no wonder she wasn't cold. Ann was in her mid to late thirties, a slim, good-looking blonde. She came across as a bit overbearing, and there was something about her that I didn't quite trust.

Ann was here to spend the week with her boyfriend Jerry, who she was now watching play a policeman in the show. You could tell they had fallen in love very recently. Ann told me they met on the Internet a year ago and the relationship had been slowly building. As well as his acting, Jerry owned his own plumbing business. Ann explained she worked as a medical examiner but also had an investigation business (as she put it: she's a spy).

At twenty-eight, Jerry has never been married, but he's been in a few long-term relationships. This seemed to be the real thing for him. An only child, he's lived in Southern California his whole life.

Ann's story was a little more involved as she married straight out of high school and had a child right away. Even though she knew her marriage was failing, she went on to have two more children, three sons, the oldest being twelve now. She described her ex as "pretty much a loser". Prior to meeting Ann, he had been married briefly before and had a child. That child was put up for adoption and the marriage dissolved.

Her husband was a handsome Navy man, and Ann had high hopes, but he chased other women from the start. They divorced three years ago, and he remarried three weeks later. His new wife wanted a child and so he went to the doctor and had a vasectomy reversed. Ouch! But fortunately she didn't conceive and this third marriage ended eight months later.

After she got divorced, Ann went on a dating spree. The court awarded joint custody of her three sons even though her ex was so strict with the children, they were often very unhappy when they were with him. For example, Ann got a call from the school nurse saying that her nine year old son had been abused. His father had hit him because he got a B- on a test. Back to court, but joint custody still prevailed.

Ann and Jerry wanted to marry. She was sure his parents loved her and she felt the same way about them even though she lived a thousand miles away. But it was not so easy to accomplish. Jerry did not want to leave the area for various reasons. He was an only son with strong family ties locally. He was also deeply committed to his plumbing business, and wouldn't let down his employees and their families by moving. She couldn't leave Wisconsin with her children due to the joint custody situation, so she thought the only alternative was for him to move. Why was I not surprised?

Ann and Jerry were not in a tearing rush, and I was sure they'd eventually marry and have their own family. As the half-hour dinner break ended, Jerry went back to work on the set as a policeman and Ann watched him go in the chill evening. "I think I'll have to go inside," she said, ending our chat. She handed me her business card for her investigation business. Ann operated under an alias, "Wanda the Wizard". She told me it was a thriving business. In case I ever needed anyone investigated, she said I should call her. As we parted and said good-bye, she turned around to me and said, "Oh, by the way, what's your name?"

7

Tom

Working as a stand-in could be pretty tedious work. Stand-ins do exactly that: they stand in for the stars while all the lighting and marks are being set. It was the ideal job for someone who could just patiently follow instructions: "stand here; move right, one step back." The days were very long for stand-ins: they needed to be there from the first shot of the day till the last. Then, when the stars finally arrived on the set, the stand-ins had to explain to them all their camera angles, movements and gestures. It was never my favorite job, but occasionally Casting needed a last-minute replacement as a stand-in, and for me it did make a change from the stress-inducing wrangling role.

As a stand-in, there was often a lot you could learn, not only about the job, but about the people doing it. One day I was standing in along with a boy, or shall I say a young man, named Tom. I thought he was probably in his early 20's, but he looked very young. At the end of our day, he told me he was turning thirty and freaking out at the onset of middle age. Then he told me I looked very tired. What a punk!

While we were sitting (or standing) for thirteen hours together, he told me that he had just moved from New Orleans. He was a survivor of Hurricane Katrina and had stayed alone in his house for five days until he was eventually rescued. There had been almost five feet of water in the house but fortunately he was tall, plus he'd had enough food to survive. After he was rescued by a police boat, he took another boat back and stayed in the city to help rescue other people. He came out to California about two months later and was torn about moving back.

Tom had traveled back and forth three times between California and New Orleans, helping people to rebuild their lives, while trying to find a new life for himself out west. At this point he wasn't even sure where in California he wanted to live.

He was very quiet for a few hours and then told me that he had almost died a few months before. He had been holding onto a car going thirty miles an hour while skateboarding, and then lost control and fell. He fractured his skull and was in a coma for two weeks. Slowly he came to and he has had to relearn many things, such as physical coordination and certain aspects of speech, as well as going through rehab for a broken shoulder. He had lost his sense of smell and he needed a lot of sleep every night. He claimed his party days were over. I wasn't sure I believed that.

Tom's hospital stay did have a bright side. He fell in love at the hospital with one of the nurses. Thinking further, he explained that maybe it wasn't love, perhaps it was just lust, but he did like her. So now that was something else to factor into his decision, whether to stay in California or go back to New Orleans. He told me he has to be very careful in his activities and not take any chances because after all he had fractured his skull. When I asked him if he had skateboarded again, he said of course he had. He changed the subject when I asked if he wore a helmet.

At the end of the day, they asked him to come back the next day to stand in again, but he would have to wear slacks and a button-down shirt. Problem!! He didn't even own that. Tom's entire wardrobe was T-shirts and jeans. So his acting career has been cut short.

When I said goodbye and told him to be careful, he looked at me for a few seconds. We both knew that was unlikely.

8

Renata

I'd met Renata early on during the filming of this show. She was a very pretty woman in her mid 20's. She was originally from Germany and had been in this country for three years. When I met her, she had been in a serious relationship for about six months with a man who was working as an actor on another show. They lived together and seemed very much in love. She was anxious for this relationship to work, after the disastrous experience of her marriage to Jeff, her first husband.

Renata had arrived in this country as an art student, and lived in New York. While she enjoyed being a visitor, her goal was to stay and make a new life. She met Jeff on the Internet and felt she had found her true love. He was a corporate executive, originally from the South, but living in the suburbs of Chicago at the time they met online. When she finished her art course after a year, she went there to meet him and hopefully get married. She wanted to live "the American dream". Of course, things did not go as planned, but she did the best she could.

They did get married in Chicago. Other than her husband, she knew nobody else there at the time. Part of her motivation was simply that she wanted to stay in this country. Being married to an American would give her citizenship. It didn't take long for problems to emerge. Jeff was not nice to her and became very possessive. Renata had no car so she really couldn't get around or establish an independent life. As time went on, he became verbally abusive and her life was getting worse every day. Even so, she emailed her family that things were fine because she was ashamed of her situation. Any pretence of maintaining a real marriage had soon disappeared and then she found out that he had a very serious girlfriend.

Jeff was transferred to California and when they arrived he pretty much left her to fend for herself. Renata wanted to work, but as she had nothing but a few acting courses under her belt as training, it wasn't going to help her find a steady job. In any case, Jeff would not let her work and she still had no car: she was effectively a prisoner in her house once again. It didn't take long for him to find a new girlfriend. She had to pretend she was not mad, as by now she was afraid to rile him.

She began researching how to get a divorce, while trying to keep the whole process very low key so as not to provoke more verbal or physical violence. She discovered that if she filed the case in Jeff's original home town in Tennessee, she could complete the proceedings herself. Jeff thought he wouldn't need to oppose this, because he believed Renata would never have the initiative to manage a complicated legal process.

Given that English is her second language, Renata struggled to understand the legal terms of the divorce papers. As she was working through the divorce proceedings she discovered that in addition to the girlfriend, he also had an ex-wife in Tennessee. This woman was now in jail for drug trafficking and Jeff also had a four year old daughter, whose whereabouts were unknown.

Renata kept the divorce proceedings moving along. She realized that she was indeed going to have to travel to this small town in Tennessee to get the divorce finalized. She bought her tickets to Memphis where she was told she would have to take the train and then a bus to get to this small town. She was also concerned about the "omen" of the divorce date, June 6th, 2006. Expressed as 6/6/06, she worried that it was the "666" sign of the devil. Despite worrying about this omen, she believed in her heart this was going to work out.

One piece of research she hadn't done well was the transportation. She arrived in Memphis airport late at night and found there were no buses or trains to take her the last eighty miles. In the early hours of the morning, she finally found a cab and explained her predicament to the nice old man who was driving her. He took pity on her and drove her there for $250 roundtrip, half of the regular price.

Renata was a wreck, but she knew she had to end this mess. After a long drive, her cab driver took her directly to the courthouse, where she waited for them to open. Court officials told her that her case would be heard later that day, and that when she came back at the set time, she'd be first in line. When she came back at the time they suggested, they had forgotten and she was tenth in the line. After the ninth person, there was a blackout, but she begged the judge to sign her papers to complete the divorce, which he did. The cab driver started the long drive back, but insisted on stopping at his friend's house first for a meal. Of course, she was skeptical, but what was she going to do? For once it turned out fine: Renata said she had the best spareribs she'd ever tasted. She finally got to the airport, missed her connecting flight, but eventually got back to California.

Jeff was furious. He had actually thought that she would not go through with it. He started to harass her and she had to get a restraining order. He finally stopped after he got tangled up in yet another legal problem: he found out he had another child from a high school romance and he was being brought up on charges of abandonment and failure to answer a court order.

Renata was now planning to move to Los Angeles, hoping for her big career break. Having grown up as the "beautiful blonde" trained to be the perfect wife, she had learned her life lessons the hard way and she was proud of what she had accomplished. When she did eventually speak to her parents, they asked her about Jeff. She told them that they had divorced because it just didn't work out. She spared the details of Jeff's life and her traumatic experiences. Renata decided to keep this to herself, as she thought it might upset her parents just a bit.

9

Emily

Emily and I were waiting to go on the set where we were shooting a restaurant scene in a location meant to look like Beverly Hills. She was an attractive woman in her early sixties and very well put together.

Emily started the conversation by telling me about her wedding. It was her mother's dream come true. Five hundred people attended the event which took place in a huge church in Michigan. That was forty years ago but even now when she thought about it, it still made her angry and resentful, especially considering the outcome of her marriage. She went along with the marriage to get out of her mother's house, where her father hit her mother on a regular basis, and at times took a whack at her too.

After escaping into marriage in her early twenties, her husband proved to be a big disappointment. He was unable to communicate with her or with anybody else around him. She was very lonely all the time. Her husband was not anxious to have a child, but Emily persevered. It took her four years to conceive. She miscarried twice, and finally had a son. Two years later her husband walked out the door. He was never a presence in his own son's life. Emily was devastated, and on top of that, her mother never forgave her for the failure of the marriage. Her husband had wanted out from the start. In hindsight, she claimed he's the kind of man she wouldn't mind meeting at her current stage of life: someone who would leave her alone but just be there as a partner.

Emily has had a very varied life. She traveled extensively with her son while he was growing up. She spent a lot of time in Italy and was engaged twice to two different Italian men. She said that both men had become very possessive after they'd established a sexual relationship, and she was not one to take orders. She walked out on both engagements . . . . but she kept the rings!

Her son left home at eighteen and didn't have much contact with her after that. This was another blow and she was on her own again. She once again reinvented herself: she joined the police and was on the force for eleven years. Two of them she spent on active patrol. She was promoted and then spent nine years working deep undercover. Her job was exposing drug dealers. She enjoyed her role very much but the job took a toll and as a woman, it was hard for her to advance as fast as her male colleagues and eventually she quit the force.

Emily then became a card dealer and has worked all over the world. She still worked as a dealer about three times a month, often at private parties or dinner cruises. She owned twenty tuxedos, each one designed slightly differently. Emily said she has always loved to dress up. In her sixties, she knew she was still attractive and sexy. As I looked at her face, I could tell she had been a beautiful woman in her youth.

While she now worked as a card dealer when she was not being an extra, there was another side to her life. She volunteered at a shelter to help battered women and children. I was sure that her warmth was welcomed. From her own experiences growing up, she knew first-hand what it was like to be beaten. She had a lot of insight in trying to help people rebuild their lives.

As we were talking, tears came to her eyes. She was still hurt that her only son, who was now thirty-six, got married a couple of years ago and didn't even tell her. The bride's mother knew all about it, but Emily was cut out.

She rarely saw her son and daughter-in-law. She told me her daughter-in-law didn't speak to her, but I never found out why. Emily only met her daughter-in-law at a Christmas party a year after the marriage. Her son didn't live that far away but Emily had been pretty much excluded from any relationship with them. When her daughter-in-law got pregnant, her son didn't even tell her until she was almost five months along. Her daughter-in-law remained very close to her own family and her husband seemed to go along with this.

Emily tried to get closer to them again and arranged a baby shower for about twenty people at her home in California. Her son and daughter-in-law were going to attend, but they canceled the day before the event. The reason her son gave was that his wife was too tired to travel because of the impending birth, even though the baby wasn't due for another three months.

Emily's grandson was now eight months old and she had no hope of seeing him anytime soon, but Emily was a survivor. She dried her eyes as we went back to work and took our place as patrons in the Beverly Hills restaurant. She looked right at home.

10

Donna

At age nineteen, she said her goal was to make people laugh, so loud and so hard that they cured cancer. She really told me that.

Donna hadn't planned to become a star, but her high school teacher told her that she was one of the most talented actresses that she had ever met. The teacher also told her that she had a friend at Harvard Drama School who would give her a free scholarship for four years. I supposed it was just a minor point that there was no such place as Harvard Drama School.

Donna was looking into going into big business eventually. She was not sure what kind, but she didn't intend to stay in her current job at a karaoke bar and strip club for the rest of her life.

She lived at home with her parents, who were still unmarried. She really loved her mother and regarded her as her best friend. Her dad was a hardcore drug addict and after much therapy, he was now only smoking pot and snorting coke. He had been living on disability since falling off a ladder while working as a painter. Soon they'd be joined in their small three-bedroom house by her grandfather.

Donna was looking forward to moving into a new room which she was planning to design to match the pink dye that she now had running through her long black hair. Her hair was naturally blonde. In fourth grade her mother started putting highlights in it to brighten her up. Now dyed black, her hair covered part of her bare midriff which was hanging over her way-too-tight jeans: she could have afforded to lose a little weight.

Donna was planning to go to Oregon to "kidnap" her best friend and bring him back to California. He moved up there to support his mother who was a drug addict, as was his father. However, he has been happy there, working at an automotive store, but she felt very strongly that this was not the right place for him. She talked endlessly, and never came up for breath. I was sure that she was smoking something other than cigarettes whenever she left the set.

This set was looking very, very messy by this time. When we had arrived, it looked horrible, so ten hours later you could just use your imagination. People were not only sleeping but snoring. Some were playing games, others talking or eating, all stretched out all over the place—it actually looked very much like an airport terminal where all flights had been canceled for the past two days. It was now four in the morning and we'd been here since two in the afternoon the day before. It was still ninety degrees, and the air conditioner was leaking water near the electrical cables. Tempers were flaring and there were a lot of intense whispered conversations going on.

There was still another scene to shoot. The restaurant scene was over, and some of the patrons in the restaurant now needed to be "recycled" to be young and very hip party-goers. This was a tough challenge for Wardrobe. Looking at the remaining extras, I thought it was going to be unlikely they'd find anyone even remotely resembling what they wanted. They started by looking for someone young. Donna was certainly young enough, but could she really be recycled as trendy? Not my problem: I was already out the door.

11

Lucinda

It would be hard not to spot her. Lucinda had gone through an amazing transition since I met her a little under a year before. At first she was polite, well mannered, dressed nicely and was giving out a Mormon Bible to anyone who would take it. I refused, as did virtually everyone else. A slim, attractive girl in her mid-twenties, she had light brown hair and a beautiful complexion. Lucinda had been married for four years. From what I'd heard, her husband was a very nice man who was quite dedicated to her. Her main hobby was sewing and she made everything she wore. Aside from being a dedicated Mormon, she had a very successful Avon business. If you sat next to her, you had probably been approached many times about becoming a customer.

In the beginning she wore clothes that were tight but not too revealing. She had a great body, but after we had been working for about six months, much less of it was covered by clothing. Over the same period, her religious fervor diminished, her bible disappeared and she became quite a flirt. Who knew where all that energy came from? Maybe drugs? As I said, her Mormon values were all gone.

Lucinda started hanging out with the crew and going to parties with different actors, and anybody else who was around. When other women her age asked about her husband, she explained to them that he was a very quiet man and it was okay with him. It was fine, her husband had said, to go out and party a bit. But she seemed to be going out until about four in the morning and she was either at a party or in bed with someone.

By this time, about eight months into the shooting of the show, the group in our "extras holding area" had become very divided. The girls that had originally been friendly with her left her in the dust, so now Lucinda had to find a new group. This took her no time at all. She found a group of women who were unattached in terms of boyfriends. This was a crowd that "ran", and all of whom were very, very sexy. Lucinda had found her new niche.

These girls were booked every day for their looks alone. Most didn't last because they felt this work was beneath them. They seemed to look at me as an example of someone who'd been doing this so long that I now appeared to them like the "maiden aunt" of the extras. Now that Lucinda had taken up with her new crowd, her old group was constantly saying how horrible she was, and always complained to me about her.

Lucinda herself started complaining that I didn't let her make as much money as she should. In fact, this was largely out of my control but as the wrangler in charge of extras, I preferred to place those extras in scenes on the set who were more reliable and less inclined to give me a hard time. At times Lucinda was late to work and then sometimes fell asleep on arrival. Of course, everyone sucked up to me. I never knew why they bothered because they knew I always tried to be fair to all, but there were moments when my patience was tested.

Basically, by this point, I just couldn't stand Lucinda myself and neither could any of the other people in charge, except of course, the young male directors and producers. At one point I had to try to discipline her because her behavior was just totally against the rules. I was surprised as no-one had ever crossed me before. It started when Lucinda had a fit, complaining that I had only put her in one scene in the show rather than two. She claimed that her lack of screen time was entirely my fault. In fact, I had no control over this. She had been playing a maid and obviously the director thought that the set was clean enough. She had a meltdown. When she calmed down, she tried to apologize to me, explaining that her aunt had just died and that's why she'd been so moody. The next day she tried to use exactly the same excuse again, but told me her best friend had just died. I never could stand a liar, but someone who couldn't keep their lies straight was even worse. That day I told her I would not tolerate this, I was going to talk to the casting director and let him know.

Lucinda had made a lot of money on this show. She had no talent, had trashed her marriage in the process and I wasn't going to take a lie for an apology. I told the casting director and he said he would suspend her for two weeks. Of course, all the young girls loved the casting director. They all had his private number so they could get in touch with him at any time. By then, her former friends were complaining endlessly to him about how terrible Lucinda had been on the set. Now remember, these girls were best, best friends when this show started.

But a sexy look counts for a lot in this business. Despite all the problems, the next day she was back. The cameraman just loved looking at those tits.

12

Stories from the Group

There were fifteen people in the group I was supervising, sitting in a nearly deserted office building waiting to do our scenes as "background" on the show. Almost from the beginning the group split into two: men on one side in a row, women on the other side in a circle. In the circle there were four other women and myself, two of us "oldies" and three in their twenties.

My contemporary was a woman who had put on forty pounds in the past few years, menopause and all. I had worked with her before. Maria was a tough character, forty-nine, Mexican and married for thirty years to her high school sweetheart. They lived on nine acres about forty five minutes from where we were working. The homestead included two thoroughbred horses and three very special pure-bred dogs that were constantly entered in dog shows and winning medals. She owned a Mexican restaurant which had been in business for eighteen years. She mentioned that business had been okay but it had fallen off recently because of higher gas prices.

Maria would have liked to sell everything and move to Montana, but of course, that was just a fantasy in her mind. That couldn't happen right now. Her husband, she said, was a wonderful man and was in the construction business with their son, Juan, who just moved home after a disastrous divorce. He was married for two years and had two children. Maria knew the marriage was a mistake from the start, which was confirmed to her right before the wedding ceremony when her future daughter-in-law called her a "wicked bitch". Her daughter-in-law had a stream of boyfriends, often twice her age and she took off with them constantly. When her daughter-in-law was meant to be in charge of the children, she was generally sleeping and when they were away from her, she was doing drugs and selling various items that she and Juan acquired during their marriage. Juan was devoted to the children and had been fighting to get sole custody. For the time being, the children spent most of their time with Maria. She had arranged her house around their needs.

As I saw the tears well up in her eyes, my heart went out to her. What an awful situation. She was a very take-charge type of person, but I could see all the pain outlined in her face.

Next to her were the three younger women. First there was Anna. Her implants were literally the biggest that I had ever seen on someone who was a size 4. She was sitting next to Lexi and next to her was Elise.

Anna was a show business kid from a big Italian family, the oldest of four girls. Her mother pushed her daughters into television at a very young age and now her youngest sister was the only one involved, because she was only twelve and couldn't say no. Anna came from a strict Catholic family where sex, boys, drugs and relationships were never discussed. She was very young to be so disillusioned already. She attended a private college and really wanted to build a career, even though all her parents wanted was to become grandparents. The money she made as a child in commercials was already gone. Her mother assured her it financed her childhood career. I didn't think so.

Next up was Lexi. I'd seen her on these shoots for many months. She was 5-6, with light eyes and brown hair, and a great figure. However, she always looked a bit sad and when she started talking about her mother, she became relentless in her criticism. She had an older and younger sister. The younger sister was severely anorexic and depressed. The older was merely confused. The mother didn't even acknowledge there were problems.

Lexi had found a small growth on her arm and it turned out to be cancer. It had to be removed and now needed to be checked every six months. Her mother was diagnosed with another cancer the same day as Lexi. This was a serious blow to Lexi as well as her mother. Lexi's father lives in the shadow of her mother and she never said a word about him.

She had visions of a serious acting career, but she faced many real obstacles—money, organization, and worst of all, her parents. There were tears in her eyes as she told me about them—"the enemy". I tried to comfort her, but I knew she would be in the same situation the next time I saw her. Common sense was not one of her strong points.

Elise was next to Lexi. Her long blonde hair, slightly highlighted, hung to her waist and her mostly exposed boobs made quite an appearance. Elise started doing beauty pageants when she was seven years old and her mother never let her quit. She told me that when she was a teenager, her mother acted younger than she, always a new boyfriend, a new job, or a new home.

The only "mature" touch about her mother was the ever-present martini in her hand.

They lived in Utah and Elise was quite successful in her role as model and beauty queen. However, Elise got pregnant in her senior year of college and had a baby. She married her boyfriend who was from a strict Mormon family. She was diagnosed with a rare form of cervical cancer when she was twenty and told that she could never have another child. The baby's father was in and out of the picture, not exactly a Mormon figure, and they divorced. Elise did eventually manage to have another child with her second husband. So now at twenty-seven, she had a nine year old and a two year-old, and was dealing with two different dads. Her new in-laws despised her and called her "the bikini model who would never go away."

She was very beautiful and had been successful in her own right, but she also had been very erratic in her approach to life. She found a small bump on her back two years ago. She tried to squeeze it open, and failed, so she had her husband try, also to no avail. I suggested that she might see a dermatologist to check it out as she had had cancer before. She said she'd think about it.

While the women were chatting, one of the boys, I should say young men, was taking pictures of the group which they intended to put on My Space. An older man approached me, one of the extras. We'd worked together many times before; he's in his sixties, gray-haired, distinguished-looking but with an outsized ego. For the fifth time he told me how he went to Harvard, got his master's degree from Wharton and used to fly to Washington weekly to do very special, important jobs in the White House. He told me he made millions, but I've heard this story from him too many times before. He told me he just cashed in some stocks and put $200,000 into CD's. Why he needed to talk about this on a set where everybody was making $140 a day was very inconsiderate in my view.

He started telling me about his investments and how smart men could really do very well in business if they had enough drive like himself. He said he could not stand doing this job anymore, standing outside in ninety degree heat and being treated poorly for ten hours a day. I still didn't understand why he was doing it, but there had to be some reason: I assumed there must have been something he wasn't telling me.

In his spare time, he made various decorative ornaments for the house. He has made hundreds of them and had a buyer in San Francisco who bought them all the time, providing him with a good profit. He told me that he had recently given his wife a large sum of cash to buy anything she wanted, but then explained that he had strongly suggested she not spend it and put it into a savings account instead. Who knows what makes a marriage work? He assured me the show would be using many more of us "older people" in the next few weeks, even including me. Thanks.

After he left, a man named Devlin came over and started to talk to me. He told me he had an IQ of 156. This was discovered when he was four. At seven, his musical talent was discovered when he was playing Mozart. He was now in his late fifties. Well, he might have been a brilliant man but he seemed to have done everything in his power to negate this during his life.

After graduating Yale at eighteen, Devlin decided to pursue nothing, much to the chagrin of his Mayflower descendant parents. He claimed that his great-great uncle was Sam Houston, of "Houston, Texas" fame. Devlin roamed the country and hooked up with a very wealthy woman even though he admitted she had "no class". They moved out to the West Coast and she had a baby and then promptly fell in love with someone else. Devlin did not see his daughter much after that. He said the child's mother had poisoned her mind with horrible tales of her father and there was never any contact between father and daughter. His ex-wife died of cancer two years ago and Devlin's reaction was, "what goes around, comes around."

His daughter was now living with the mother's stepsister who had reinforced the barriers between Devlin and the girl. He said he hoped to have a real father-daughter relationship with her one day, but if he doesn't, he doesn't. In appearance, he resembled a nutty professor and was one of the thinnest men I have ever seen. He told me he wins every single audition he goes on but somehow he was just never quite picked for the great roles. While we were waiting, he started to try to psycho-analyze me. I merely turned to him and said, "Don't you dare." I probably just confirmed his hatred for women.

As the time was going on, more extras had arrived, and it turned out that one of the new, very young, college-age girls was being harassed by another extra, a man in his forties. I didn't realize this at first. However, after a number of us returned to the set after dinner, we found her in hysterics. I asked her what the problem was, and eventually she calmed down enough to explain that the older man had started with verbal abuse, and then had started throwing spit-balls at her. Nobody had intervened or helped her. Even worse, there were two other extras dressed as cops plus a real security guard in the room when this guy started harassing her. These three men watched this whole thing going on and did nothing. By this time the girl was hysterical, and the three women and I tried to calm her down as much as we could. Understandably she was a wreck.

The guy got fired. He was ethnically an Asian Indian and subsequently decided to accuse the director of being a racist. It turned out that he had been blacklisted due to problem behavior in the past, but changed his hair and general appearance in order to get right back on the set under another name.

Overtime would start after nine hours. At eight hours and fifty-six minutes, we wrapped for the day. It was a weary group of extras who straggled out the door looking for the studio shuttle for the mile-long ride to the parking lot.

13

Patricia

Patricia said "Hi" and began to talk to me even before I had put my coffee cup down. We were standing around waiting to get into our wardrobe for the day. She told me she had three sons. From her appearance, I guessed she must have been in her late sixties. That day she was playing a patient in an unnamed New Jersey hospital where I was playing a visitor at her bedside.

Patricia told me her mother was one of eleven girls and one boy, and her father was also one of eleven. She went into a nunnery at age fifteen and re-entered the outside world fifteen years later. She told me that even though she was thirty then, she still had the energy of a teenager and was in good shape both mentally and physically. A priest, who was also a family friend, had helped her make the difficult transition back to the outside world.

She was living on the East Coast, and with $500 in her pocket she drove across the country in three days. She ended up in Northern California where she settled down, got married and went back to school. Eventually she graduated with her Masters in English.

She taught in California for thirty years before moving to the southern part of the state five years ago. Here, she was overqualified for most teaching jobs so the pay she had been offered was much less than she was used to in her old job. As a result, Patricia had not been teaching, and said her life had become very lonely. She had moved down here for her husband's job, and didn't really know many people.

Patricia's three sons were separated by just sixteen months each, and they all have enjoyed a close relationship, with each other and with her. One of her sons had a good job as an air traffic controller, based in Kansas. He had two daughters, five and three. The daughter-in-law really didn't like her. She claimed Patricia spent too much time trying to take her son away from her, even though they lived over a thousand miles apart. When she visited them she stayed at a hotel, not at their home. She kept her mouth shut when her daughter-in-law complained about how expensive everything was, leaving out that she had just had a tummy tuck and a boob job before she was even thirty.

Another son had become an artist and he lived in Queens, New York. He had been compared to Chagall and his works lined all the walls of his home: he was another one just waiting to be discovered. To make a living he worked for the New York City Public School system, helping out in programs for mentally-challenged children. She was convinced that it was only a matter of time before he was discovered as an artist.

Her third son was having a hard time. He had enlisted in the military right out of high school and had been in the service for twelve years. He had just got back from Iraq and was in bad shape. While he was in the service, his wife had left him and had taken their only son, then three years old, who was very attached to him. The boy was now six, and his wife had moved in with her new boyfriend. She now had a three year old with the boyfriend. The last time he came to pick up his son, she literally tried to run him over in her car. She wanted him out of the way. Patricia's heart was broken over this, but it seemed that they have a very tortured relationship.

She spoke to this son on the phone many times during the day. She was angry that he had spent a lot of money on an SUV which turned out to be expensive to run, as well as to buy. On her third call to him she told him that another extra on the show had just bought eleven acres of land in the desert for $25,000. She asked why he couldn't do something like that.

I happened to know that the extra who bought this land lives on a trailer there with no water or electricity. He was hoping that a highway would be built there and the government would pay him a lot of money for his property. Well, that could be a story for another day.

14

Holly

We were shooting a major party scene. As extras, we had to make it seem realistic, so we all had to keep moving around every few minutes. In some ways it was just like a real party, except that on camera everyone got along.

When Holly sat down next to me she said she was just like any other twenty-three year-old girl . . . . except that she took her leg off at night. She had developed cancer in her lower leg when she was eleven, one of the only thirteen cases reported in medical history. She'd almost died from the chemo and radiation. They'd tried everything to save her leg. She had a bone marrow transplant which left her in an isolation ward at the hospital for over a month, but eventually, her leg had to be amputated. Holly was a very, very positive person, with an amazing outlook on life. She was very spiritual which had helped her maintain her positive attitude.

As well as working on this show, Holly was on the "special ops" unit. The studio complex had an adjacent area which was set up as a simulated Iraqi village. This was used to help prepare soldiers for their tour in Iraq, using extras to play Iraqi villagers and insurgents. To make this as realistic as possible, the casting units hired amputees (common in Iraq due to the war). Holly had been a regular member of that group. She said that she and the others on the special ops unit were dedicated to this work and were very proud of their contribution. Everyone on the set was certainly very fond of her and she had been a great asset to the team.

The year that she got cancer, her mother ran away at Christmas-time, and took all of the Christmas presents. Her father then banned her from any contact with Holly. She got through the whole cancer ordeal with no relationship with her mother. Now Holly said they are best friends. She said her mother was seriously disturbed at the time, but she did not go into details. I guessed that the running away was probably the least of it.

Holly grew up on a farm in Missouri and came from a family of boys. She was the only girl. At the time we spoke, she had thirteen brothers and one more on the way. Of those, only three were from the same parents. Her parents have both remarried, so the other ten were step or foster children who had now become part of the family: either being adopted or in various stages of becoming a more permanent part of the group.

Their farm was very isolated, miles away from any town. Every morning Holly would go out, get the eggs that had been laid overnight and milk the cows. She had to grow up very self-reliant, which had given her real strength and independence.

After her amputation, Holly was home-schooled which she didn't like at all. She married very young, at eighteen, and the marriage was a disaster. Her husband abused her terribly, both mentally and physically. I guessed she stayed because she felt she deserved no better. She got pregnant which itself was a miracle, because the doctor said she would never be able to conceive after all the chemo and radiation. Her husband subsequently pushed her down the stairs and she lost the baby three months into the pregnancy. She finally ended the marriage and now has had a new boyfriend for the past two months.

Holly was very positive about her future. She had decided she wanted to be an actress and that she had the necessary talent and dedication. After what she had lived through, no challenge should be too daunting for her.

15

Bobby

At six foot two, 200 pounds and with beautiful mahogany skin, Bobby was a real presence. He had big brown eyes with a twinkle in them. Bobby was one of twelve children. He was born in California and when he was thirteen, his grandmother decided it was time to move the family to North Carolina for a better life. It was Bobby's grandmother, not his mother, who was the driving force in this family and so the family moved. Bobby was devastated, but his best friend's mother offered to adopt him so he could stay and continue his education in California.

His family had all gone back to North Carolina, but he stayed and finished high school in California. Only one other of his six brothers had ever graduated from high school in his family. The others had all dropped out. Bobby was now twenty-five and his mother already has had nineteen grandchildren, even though only two of her children were married.

Bobby was always interested in theater and appeared in many high school and local productions. Now he was trying to get his first real acting job. He and his friend used to sell shoes at Nordstrom and competed to see who could sell the most in a single hour. Bobby said that his friend always won by a lot because "he was the best bullshitter" Bobby had ever met.

Bobby seemed to have tremendous confidence in himself but was generally pretty quiet. This was the end of our third twelve-hour day in a row. As the director called "wrap," we looked at each other and smiled, knowing that we'd both be back the next day. Bobby had been waiting patiently for his scene as the bartender for three days, just sitting there. Once again, he knew tomorrow would be the day that would start his long career.

16

Families Untied

Many of the conversations on set focused on family problems. Some of my extras came from broken homes, others had pretty much broken their homes themselves. Once that cycle had established itself, it could be hard to stop: more often than not, children grew up and recreated what they knew, or had been used to. I've touched on this in many of the stories in this book, and honestly, some of the victims of these broken homes didn't even know how to try to get back on track. On the other hand, there were some who clearly were trying, even if it didn't always work.

Lenny was one guy in my regular extra group. He had one child with his current wife and two with his first wife. It didn't stop there: his ex-wife then had a three year-old with no dad in the picture. Lenny had become very attached to this girl, and he helped them out financially. In turn, his ex had two sons from her first marriage before he met her. All in all, he was involved in family arrangements with six kids. It was a strain on his finances, but he made a point of living up to his responsibilities.

Samantha was another one with kid problems. She was middle-aged, and seemed very intelligent and caring. She spent most of one day talking to me. She had her first child when she was seventeen. She grew up in a strict Catholic family and no-one even thought about sex, supposedly. Samantha decided to have the baby and her family threw her out. She went to work and neighbors helped her out with taking care of her son.

It was a tough life, and eventually her son grew up and married a woman who was an ex-drug addict. This girl used to be an accountant, but her life had become a mess, and she was now unemployed. Samantha's son worked security on a 10:00 p.m. to 10:00 a.m. shift, four days a week. He and his wife lived in a studio and between them had three kids, ages two, six and seven. The place where they were living was a dump and the kids had been growing up in very disturbing conditions. Their father blamed his mother (Samantha), saying he grew up in a terrible situation, insisting his lack of responsibility was his mother's fault.

His wife (Samantha's daughter-in-law) has also had a difficult life. She and her sister were deserted as toddlers by their parents and had to live with a family friend. The sister was born with deformed arms and the parents were unable or unwilling to cope. Eight years later, when the girls were ten and eleven, this adoptive mother left her husband and moved in with another woman. Before they were teenagers, the girls had lost two mothers. Before she met up with Samantha's son, Samantha's daughter-in-law had two children, who by now lived with their father. Samantha's son didn't find this out till after he had married her. The two kids didn't live with them, but he still felt some responsibility towards them.

As Samantha took me through this complicated story, late in the same day, Amy came over and said she was sick. At 5'1" and maybe ninety-five pounds she looked like a waif. She seemed about to faint and she was crying. She told me that her boyfriend had constantly been abusing her verbally. I asked her why she was still with him and she said he had rescued her when her van broke down. She'd been living in it around California on and off for three years after leaving home when her parents split up and neither wanted the "burden" of looking after her. She was now living with her boyfriend's family. They didn't like her either: her career, her hold over their son, or her looks. She and her boyfriend had a joint checking account and she was afraid to leave because he was threatening her that he'd keep all her money. She called her mother and step-father in Florida who told her she had got herself into all this trouble and now she could get herself out. Her real father had money, but she wouldn't go to him because she hated him, and she was afraid that he was abusing her stepsister.

Amy was requested on the set all the time. A strikingly beautiful girl, she had been sleeping with one of the directors. He liked to have her on the set all day because of her appearance; it was now my job to find him and tell him that she had to leave. He was fifty-one, she was twenty-two. Everybody knew they were an "item". What he didn't know was that she was also having sex with one of the extras. Since we worked at least twelve hours a day, I couldn't imagine the logistics of this, but after all, she was young and usually energetic!

However, she looked so sick by now, I thought she was going to pass out and I told her she could go. She had no car, so she called a friend to pick her up; she told me she might leave town and try to start over. She knew she had to try to sort her life out, but I wondered if she had already gone too far off-track. Even so, as she sat in front of me crying and shivering, my heart went out to her, as she had been driven from one bad family situation to another.

17

Eileen

I had worked with Eileen many times before and was happy to see her when I arrived on the shoot. The scene called for us to be patrons at an outdoor café and Eileen and I were at a table together. She was in her mid-fifties, and must have been very attractive in her younger days. However, she seemed to have aged a lot since I last saw her a few months ago. She said to me, "Don't ask me how I am. My daughter died of a severe asthma attack." She said she did not want to talk about it. In fact she didn't want to talk about anything. She was silent for two hours.

When she did finally decide to talk, she explained that she was in the process of leaving her boyfriend "for the fifteenth time". She was now trying to pack up her stuff to put into storage. She'd been living with this man in a very tumultuous relationship for eight years. It was just the two of them, living in a massive six-bedroom house. I couldn't understand why the relationship had persisted this long. In reality, he was very insensitive but she seemed to feel that this was what she deserved.

Her parents had been married for sixty years. Her father always had a drinking problem but her mother stuck by him. At least he had never hit her. Eileen's sister married a man who turned out to be a drug addict. He was literally killing himself in front of his family, but she too stuck by him and wouldn't leave. Eventually he died of an overdose, which didn't surprise Eileen.

Over twenty years ago, Eileen had two daughters in a long-term relationship, but she never did marry the father of these children. She left him when her daughters were eight and five, and he had not been in their lives that much since then. Sometimes he dropped in but Eileen says that basically she could never count on him. He went on to marry, divorce, marry again, and then divorce again. He did have one daughter with his most recent wife but had not been involved in her life either.

Eileen's older daughter had suffered from asthma since she was a child, and at times it seemed to be well under control. However, she had a severe asthma attack four months ago, and died five days later at age twenty-four. She was on a respirator for those last days, but never recovered. Eileen had been very close to both her daughters. The father came to his daughter's funeral, but he still remained an outsider in the lives of Eileen and her remaining daughter.

While we were talking, her phone rang. It was her lawyer saying that her trial date had been postponed. She had a lawsuit against the county, because a clerical mistake led to the police evicting her from the house where she had lived for twelve years. She was not enthusiastic about having to pursue a lawsuit, but felt she must carry through to clear her name. She had already spent a substantial sum on legal bills, and said that all of her credit was ruined.

When I complimented her on her car, she told me it was a rental. Someone had recently rear-ended her on the freeway. She was not sure whose fault it had been. Throughout the conversation, sadness seemed to seep from her pores. While we were talking, she broke into tears a number of times. I told her I would come over to help her pack if she really wanted to leave her boyfriend. She jumped at the idea, not that she wanted any help packing, but she just wanted me to be there. She had been to many grief counselors and while it helped a bit, it could never relieve the pain.

While we were talking she brought up something that she was struggling to cope with. When people asked her how many children she had, she always found herself stunned. "What do I say? I have one, but I really had two." She said there should be a generic name that you give to a child if they'd died. She didn't know what to say or do and mostly she just cried.

Eventually she planned to go back to Minnesota and live with her parents for a year or so. She just wanted to escape for a while. Her parents were fragile, but she felt she just needed to be away from everything. Her other daughter would join her. The bond between the two of them was now airtight.

The director yelled "Cut." I realized that we'd been talking this whole time on a quiet set, even though we weren't supposed to be. Eileen left me wondering how you survive life tragedies like the one she's gone through.

18

Day 35

As I drove to work I knew it would be a long day. It was a good thing that I didn't know just how long. With a lot of extras coming to the set that day, the first couple of hours were fairly chaotic, especially for me as the wrangler, but eventually we seemed to settle into some sort of order. Of course there were always problems. The wardrobe people complained that the extras brought clothes that were not only horrible, but dirty as well. As usual, the hair stylists complained that some of the extras hadn't washed their hair or that they had put in too much gel. I relayed the problems to my boss, who told me to handle them. Many of the extras failed to realize they could only be used if they dressed the way the show had requested. Already, one or two people had been let go for those reasons, and more would follow.

The caterer came over to say hello to me. We seemed to be the only two people on the set who cared whether the extras got anything to eat during the day. I had checked in thirty extras so far and I knew I had at least thirty more coming in the next hour.

I was sitting with a security guard next to me for the day. It was ten in the morning but there had been a lot of theft in the studios recently, so he was just making his presence known early in the day. When I was in charge of sixty people, it was always nice to have someone with a badge to help keep order. He had a strong presence and with him sitting there, the extras didn't try to push me around as much. He told me he was disgusted with the attitudes of some of the extras. Certainly some of them acted like spoiled brats while making a lot more money than he was. So, for much of the time he sat and watched his DVD's with his headphones on low. He didn't speak much, either to me or anyone else. Eventually Susanna came over; she was his backup security guard and she never stopped talking, which at times was more annoying than her colleague's silence.

At forty-two years old, Susanna has had four children with three different fathers. She had been married only once. The father of two of her kids was in jail. She described the other two dads as "missing in action". She said there was no point in looking for them as she didn't even know for sure who they were. Her parents had custody of her two youngest children who were five and ten, and she shared custody of her third daughter with her parents. Her oldest was an eighteen year old boy, and she claimed she managed okay with him. Her mother was pretty busy. As well as looking after the two young girls, she also had custody of two children belonging to Susanna's brother. He was married to a twenty-two year-old who was now pregnant. He was forty and his ex-wife was in jail.

Susanna switched topics frequently. Later at lunch she said she was amazed how much I could eat. I was eating a salad with chicken and fresh vegetables. She must have outweighed me by almost fifty pounds and was a couple of inches shorter. She claimed she could never eat that much and attributed my appetite to a "hollow leg". I preferred my other security guard even though he didn't speak to me much.

When another group of extras arrived, I knew at least one of them was going to be a big problem. Antonia had on a gold sequined dress that was two sizes too small and had a slit up to her ass. She was about fifty pounds overweight so that didn't help either. On top of that she was hysterical crying when she arrived and she wouldn't tell me why. Eventually I calmed her down and sent her to Wardrobe, but I knew they'd be calling me on this one. Wardrobe fitting was meant to take about ten minutes, but after twenty Antonia still hadn't re-appeared. During that time I had checked in twenty more extras. Even compared to the early morning crowd, they looked pretty bedraggled at this point, but at least they had showed up. The shooting script needed even more extras for the evening scenes, but finding them was not my problem.

Antonia was now crying over in Wardrobe but at least she had been put into a different outfit. A voice then screamed into my Walkie-talkie that the boys from Brown had arrived in the 14-seat Hummer. I was told to be their private host. Forget about the rest of my group of extras, which still now numbered around sixty people even after some had completed their scenes and gone home. The "boys from Brown" were important people. They were guests of the Network. Suddenly the set was being cleaned and dusted, garbage pails were being emptied, and snacks were taken away, because they looked too messy and were not really in the budget anyway. They certainly hadn't cost too much: we'd mostly been given chips and some day-old bagels. All the activity could signal just one thing: the head of the Network was coming to visit.

In my new role, I greeted the boys with my Walkie-talkie in tow and it turned out they were really a pleasure to be with. All dressed up in blue blazers and khaki pants, they were an a-capella singing group representing their school and touring the country giving concerts. The head of the Network had gone to Brown and founded this group twenty years ago, so they were going to be in this episode. There was no sign of the head man yet, so the cleaning continued.

My extras had settled in, waiting for the evening scenes, sleeping, playing cards and reading movie magazines. The boys from Brown sat in a circle and started playing board games. It was a real contrast for me to talk to them as they intersected with a different aspect of my life. They knew the high school that my sons had attended and some were applying to grad school at the college where one of my sons was studying. I didn't think that they realized that the people lying on the floor snoring were actually going to be in the scene with them.

At that point I got a call on my Walkie-talkie that Antonia was still crying in Wardrobe because they had yet to find an appropriate outfit that she could wear. They were about to send her home. I went over to Wardrobe, explained the situation and we all scampered around trying to find something for her to wear.

Then I got called back to the set, where my extras were sleeping and the college boys were waiting. I was asked to bring the college boys some bottles of water. Of course there was no bottled water allocated for the extras. My Walkie-talkie squawked again. My new instructions were to "wrangle up ten attractive couples" and bring them on set. I was given exactly one and a half minutes to do this. It was not easy, but I found enough extras who vaguely fitted the description, woke them all up and got everybody onto the set. Immediately, I got a call to go back to Wardrobe. Antonia was definitely going to be sent home. She had now had a real breakdown while waiting to find some clothes as nothing fit her. I felt it was not right to send her home without any money. I found the second-second assistant director and he agreed we would give her half a day's pay, which was going to be $30.

While this was going on, the first assistant director was on the phone complaining to the casting director that they didn't like the people Casting was sending them. Not only that, but the director was getting increasingly annoyed at the slow pace of shooting. There was often tension on the set, but that day it had escalated to a point where I knew something had to give. I thought the problem of Antonia was resolved, so I mentally put it on the back burner, but immediately I got a call, or a scream rather, to bring the college boys to lunch "ASAP". They were taken to the front of the line of course, and the other hundred cast and crew didn't love the fact that the boys were getting all this special attention. Well, tough. These kids were Network VIP's for the day.

The next call was to get the young, attractive couples onto the set and get the extras back to the holding area. There was a halt in shooting because of the meal break, which I didn't even bother with as I had to get Antonia signed out and then had to pick up the college boys from their lunch. I overheard that the director had ordered ten more men as extras from Casting for a scene this afternoon, wearing tuxedos. This was a rush call: they needed them in an hour. The chances late on a Friday afternoon of finding even one respectably dressed and decent looking man was very, very slim. Forget about the tuxedos, these guys rarely had suits. At least Wardrobe wasn't my problem.

The head of the Network had arrived and was wandering around, checking on progress. He came over to my group so I introduced myself to him and we chatted for a moment. The rest of my extras had straggled back from the break. By this time it was five p.m., but our meal-times were very skewed because shooting had to start so late that day. Legally there had to be a minimum number of hours workers must be off the set before the next work-day. We had worked so late the previous night that we weren't allowed to get our usual early morning start.

The college boys came back and were by now immersed in academic journals and some very thick books. Even though they were mixed in with the extras, it seemed like they were not even in the same room.

I was starting to lose my voice which was frustrating since "screaming time" had just begun. I got a call to switch channels on my Walkie-talkie, which was never a good sign. Maybe I'd done something wrong. As soon as I realized it was the first assistant director calling me, I tried to think of what problem I might have caused. When she started with the phrase, "This is Day 35 of a 61-day shoot . . . . haven't you learned anything yet?" it didn't sound too good. This time I was in trouble because I had sent Antonia home without telling the person in charge. I told her I had told the second-second assistant director, but she told me that wasn't good enough. The company was going to lose money today, paying someone not to work. They were out $30. I told her to take it out of my pay. Of course, I couldn't even imagine how much the company was spending on lunch, but OK, it was my fault.

It was around seven p.m. by now and more male extras started dragging in, dressed in their tuxedos. They had only been able to find older men, and they all had "old-style" tuxedos. Wardrobe was angry. They called me but it was too late to find anybody else. The college boys had finished their scene, and performed a short encore, singing for the cast and crew before I loaded them back in their 14-seat Hummer. The head of the Network was in the front seat. The boys thanked me profusely and offered to put in a good word for me.

Back to my people: I performed a quick reality check. They were getting tired after doing nothing all day. As soon as I sat down, one of the stable of "eye-candy" extras came running over (they're called that because they're the good-looking ones that the director liked to have on the set all the time). There was an emergency with her friend Ellie in the back. I loved these girls because they were very sweet to me, but there was definitely a panic attack going on. One look at a hysterical Ellie and I knew this went way beyond the set. I learned that her father-in-law had just had a massive heart attack and was being rushed to the hospital. It didn't sound good. Her in-laws lived about an hour and a half away. I told her she had to go home and accompany her husband to the hospital. I let her go immediately, knowing that this serious a medical situation would probably have a bad ending. Since her marriage was a bit shaky, she really had to go. I assured her that tonight would not be the night that she would have been picked for a bigger part in this show.

Once I got her out, I sat back down at my makeshift desk and noticed that my silent security guard was on to a new film on his DVD player. I really did feel better with him sitting next to me. He now became my voice-piece as the extras were getting noisy, my voice was going and we still had at least four hours to go. It was now ten p.m. and finally it had gone quiet for a few minutes, after so many calls going back and forth all day long. I had dealt with calls about background, calls about lunch, calls about wardrobe, makeup, pay, it just kept going on and on. A half hour later the second-second assistant director came back and I told her about sending Ellie home. She said that was fine as long as I had got it cleared with the boss . . . . but I hadn't. It was only six hours after I got in trouble for sending Antonia home and I had done it again. I just could not believe I made the same mistake just a few hours later. I guessed I never really did learn that lesson about letting people go without permission.

I chose to call my boss on the Walkie-talkie rather than look her in the face. I was truly embarrassed. There was silence after I told her. I said that Ellie had to leave because her father-in-law was dying after a massive heart attack. She said, "Look, we all have problems and now we are short another person." Silence. Ellie was meant to be in a ball-gown at the "charity dinner" scene. I told her I would get myself into a ball gown in five minutes and fill the space, and that's exactly what I did. I raced around to my girls and to their credit, they each offered me the use of the long dresses they had brought that day. Of course, I couldn't fit into many of them since most of these girls were a size 4 slim, but I did get into something. I was literally stuffed in to this dress and fortunately I didn't have to sit down, or I would probably have split the seams. I also got my feet into a tiny pair of formal shoes, did hair and make-up in less than a minute, and as I went onto the set, my boss was there reminding me again that it was Day 35 of a 61-day shoot and hadn't I learned anything yet.

So I ran out onto the set in the low-cut ball-gown and not one person recognized me. They only knew Melissa, the middle-aged woman in jeans and sweatshirt who took care of the extras in a room far away from the talent. It was really a very odd feeling not to be recognized by people you've worked with for months. It was the first time they'd seen a more glamorous aspect of me and when the first assistant finally realized who I was, he actually said, "Oh, my God, I can't believe how good you look. This is really amazing." Now he hadn't said much to me since I started this job on Day 1, but what could I say, I had to take a compliment whenever I could get it.

Now it was really getting late. It was 11:30 p.m. and no-one was paying much attention to the script anymore. I did my bit part and the scene was over. I changed back into my sweatshirt, jeans and long underwear: it was cold as they always tried to keep the air-conditioning running to deal with the heat generated by the studio lights. At this point we started to get ready to wrap, meaning we finally would be able to send the extras home. This was a job in itself. We were sitting waiting for the instruction to sign out and it was now 1:30 in the morning. Wrapping everybody out would take at least an hour and I could not really do anything in advance until I got the instruction from the boss.

By the time it came, I had lost my voice totally, so I enlisted the help of another person to help me sign everybody out. I assigned him all the people who had given me trouble all day and I took the rest. Finally the vouchers were signed, I was alone in the room and there were just three people left in the whole studio. I had signed off on thousands of dollars. I had cost the production $30 for sending Antonia home and I saved another $90 for sending Ellie home, because I took over for her so she had not made any overtime. So all in all, they had come out ahead. Ellie's father-in-law died before she even got there and I was so glad I made her go home.

It was now two a.m., I had been here sixteen hours and I couldn't wait to get home. I hoped that "Day 36 of 61" would go better!

19

Karen

At six feet tall she stood out in the crowd. I would have estimated her age in her forties, not thirties as she claimed, but she remained an attractive-looking woman. Her ex-husband was also working on the show. Karen had been married to him for ten years when it ended. Things were okay in their lives at first, but then she began to find him cheating on her, drinking too much and such. It took her a long time to decide to get out of the marriage because her confidence level was so low, but eventually she did.

Even after her marriage was over, her luck hadn't changed. She broke her back in an accident and meantime had nowhere to live. It turned out that her ex's grandmother had no-one to be with her and was also very fond of Karen, so she invited her to move in. She was well into her eighties, in failing health and very despondent. They were good for each other until her ex-sister-in-law accused Karen of stealing all the family jewelry from that house. Everybody in the family turned on her, incited by a couple of psychics they had employed. The family insisted that Karen take a lie detector test and she failed, even though she continued to insist she was innocent.

Because of her back problem, she became hooked on painkillers. She was by then living in a friend's spare bedroom. Her ex-husband was nowhere to be found to defend her against the charges leveled by his family members. She was brought up on charges and had no money to employ a lawyer. Two months later, the jewelry was found somewhere in the house. Either the old lady had misplaced it, or she had been framed: either way, it had never been stolen in the first place.

Too late for Karen: her reputation had been ruined. With nowhere to go, no money, no credit cards, and still living in her friend's spare bedroom, she decided to make a new start in the real estate market and did quite well for herself for a number of years. She was a good salesperson, very sincere and knew what she was talking about. Then the real estate market collapsed.

Once again, she had no income and so she decided to launch an Internet shoe business. It specialized in women's shoes, size 11-16 with wide widths. She bought a number of shoes in a warehouse close-out and built a large closet made just for her "extra-size" products. She sold them on eBay for a lot of money; her main customers were transvestites. She proceeded to set up a manufacturing shoe line and made plans to run this as a full-time business.

Even so, she still had a sad aura about her. I wished we had more time to talk that day. I had a sense there was more to tell.

I didn't see Karen for a while, and then three months after she had told me her story, I found myself working alongside her ex-husband Ian. When he introduced himself, I simply smiled and said hello, rather than reveal to him that Karen had told me all about him, about his cheating, about his being a spoiled brat and drunken slob. I didn't really want to have to sit through his story, and I felt some relief when he finished for the day. Coincidentally, later that day, I ran into Karen again.

She told me that she had had a series of relationships over the past couple of years. First there had been a "long distance" lover, who was an astronaut, but he lived in Washington DC. The astronaut could not fulfill her emotional needs, and did not treat her well, as no man in her life ever had, starting with her father. She split with him and began to look for another man immediately. After a few bad dates, she found a new love, Jose.

I asked her to keep the details to herself because I really couldn't bear to listen to all the nitty-gritty. But as I sat there trying to read, she continued anyway. She fell in love with Jose at first sight. He was Mexican and was working to repeal laws that send illegal immigrants back to Mexico. She explained that his view was that everybody had a right to live in this country, especially the members of his own family. He spent his days working to make that a reality.

Jose was divorced, with an eight year-old child. Karen became very involved with his daughter. Jose and his ex-wife had joint custody. I counted myself lucky Karen did not fill me in on all the details of that divorce, as she said it was another disaster. Karen had spent the holidays with Jose's family after knowing him for only six weeks. I've seen similar situations, and from those, my experience suggested that this was usually a big mistake! However, she told me she had fit right in and that his mother loved her, even though there was very little English spoken at the table.

Karen told me she knew this was a magical relationship between her and Jose. They spent days going to homeless shelters to help people, going to court to fight for the illegal immigrants and helping people who could not speak up for themselves because they did not speak English.

The next time I worked with Karen was a few weeks later. She was so inconsolable, it was really upsetting. After two months together, Jose had dumped her. I didn't know why, but I spent much of that day listening to a blow by blow description of every emotion one could imagine.

Two weeks later she showed up to work with a twinkle in her eye again. This time she said it was the real thing. She was having an affair with one of the actors in the show and he was in the process of leaving his second wife. As the day wore on, she told me all about him: she knew that this time the chemistry was right. She could not believe her good fortune. She was sure that this man was "the one". For her sake, I hoped he was.

20

Suzanne

We had been shooting beach scenes, and I needed two more visors for the next day's shoot. Fortunately we got out early enough so I could get to the store next to the studio. Suzanne was busy with some other customers for a few minutes and then she helped me. I recognized her from a job she did with me on the show: she did extra work from time to time if she could get some time off her regular job.

She was a very pretty young woman with dark and piercing eyes, who came across as one of those "fit, super-energetic" people. We started talking as she rang up my purchase. She was born locally in Southern California, one of four children. Her father was a dentist and her mother a homemaker and they appeared to be the "Donna Reed" family. Everything seemed so perfect, especially when the family was on display at the country club and the church. She told me that in her family nobody was allowed to express any opinions and in fact everybody was pretty miserable. The residual impact worked its way through the lives of all the children.

She was the second of four children, the only girl. One of her younger brothers had been handicapped his whole life and died unexpectedly from a seizure at age sixteen. Suzanne was eighteen then. The family was away on vacation, and she said she saw twenty years drain out of her parents' faces when it happened. She had another younger brother who even now had not really recovered from this shock and her mother had very little ability left to give him any emotional help.

This one of her brothers was very bright and as soon as he graduated he moved to Chicago, basically to start a new life and get away from his family. Her older brother worked with her father and went the traditional way: married with kids. Her parents have been very pleased with that.

Four years ago Suzanne was diagnosed with a rare bone disease. She felt she was losing a lot of control of her body. Before this happened, she had been suffering from carpal tunnel syndrome and was in such pain she dropped out of college and worked at various jobs. Suzanne had worked as a dental assistant, an actress, a mortgage broker, a real estate broker, an artist and a student of Western medicine.

Due to the bone disease, her spine had to be fused because the discs had severe nerve damage. The next year a car crashed into her and finished the job on her back. She had always been a very creative person and loved to work, but still winced not only at her own pain, but at the pain that her parents were going through every day, worrying about her. They were generous with their time and money even though, as her mother pointed out, no man would want her because she was such a physical wreck. Her epidural shots for pain had been costing her about $20,000 a year but she stopped them because they weren't helping the pain enough and she felt they were not worth the money.

Suzanne was thirty but looked younger. People could never believe she had such bad problems physically because she looked so good. Suzanne could still work out, but was limited in what work she could do. Even so, she seemed to have more energy than most of the people I knew. She had a boyfriend, although her parents didn't approve of him: he was forty-eight, twice-divorced and had a child. However, Suzanne was always looking to a bright future.

As I left, I shook her hand, forgetting the carpal tunnel syndrome. She winced but then smiled. I was sure I'd see her again soon. I looked at my watch and realized she had told me this story in under fifteen minutes.

21

Society Girls

Some scenes for the show required "high society" style and appearance. While wardrobe could provide some presentable clothes, the usual twenty-something extras couldn't really carry off this look, so the call would go out for more "sophisticated types", especially if the requirement was owning their own classic-style clothes. I'd occasionally get hired in this group, but there were also a core group of other women who came in specifically for these shoots. Many were fairly wealthy, and did this more for interest than for career ambition. They wanted to tell their friends they were on TV. On this day, we were on location at a 20,000 square foot mansion where we were dressed as attendees at a high-end auction.

As we sat at our tables waiting for shooting to start, I found myself next to Cheri, whom I'd seen a couple of times before at these "high-end" scenes. Though her looks were fading a bit now she was in her late forties, she was still a classic beauty, with blonde hair and bright blue eyes. She had traveled to many countries with a variety of rich boyfriends. When she talked about it, there was a remembered excitement in her eyes.

She wasn't always in the "rich set", however. Cheri grew up as an "army brat". Her family moved almost every two years. She was the oldest of eight and her father put her in charge of the other children at the age of ten because her mother was too busy having babies. Her father was a general and there was never any emotional warmth in the house at all. Quite the opposite. Her mother was there physically, but unavailable mentally. As soon as she could, she left home and headed for Europe. She eventually married "well", at least financially, even if not emotionally. Certainly when she came back to the States as a divorcee, she had plenty of money to live on, and that worked for her.

Barbara was another one of the "society crowd". These ladies seemed to have a very selective memory. I always found it interesting when she started telling me about jobs that she had worked on, and forgot that I had been working right alongside her. She had a good imagination too. We have worked on a fair number of shoots together, and Barbara always referred to us as "the twins", because she saw us as so similar in both age and looks. I was eight inches taller and maybe fifteen years younger, so we must have made an interesting set of twins. However I resolved to keep in touch with Barbara when the show was over as she was always interesting to talk with, and a truly generous-minded person.

Unlike Cheri the "jet-setter", in the past few years it seemed that Barbara never left a ten-mile radius of her home, other than to get to work. She was independently wealthy, but I still wondered if she had ever been on a plane. She never went to movies, out to dinner, or to plays, confining herself just to her club and her weekly card game. When Barbara was in a generous mood, she would tell people what a great mother I was. She still couldn't remember if I had one or two sons (as I had told her a few times, I had three).

Cheri was usually the best dressed of this crowd. On one previous shoot, she told me she had been worried that she didn't have quite the right outfit for that day's auction scene. She had been looking for one suit in particular, but then she realized that she had given it to her maid a few weeks before. She called the maid and asked her if she was using it. When she said "no," Cheri was about to ask for it back, only the maid added that she'd given it to her sister in Mexico, who loved it. Cheri was not thrilled that she had to bring her second choice instead.

She went on to talk about her new Italian leather couch and the two matching chairs which cost $25,000 between them. I figured that a lot of people could furnish an entire house for less than that. She was sending them back to Italy because they wrinkled when you sat on them. Cheri didn't like anything that wrinkled. You could tell that by looking at her "uplifted" face.

Cheri told me she was attending a very big society wedding the next week, where hundreds of guests were being ferried by helicopter to the top of a mountain in Tahoe. She was a bit put out that she hadn't been invited to an even bigger "society event" that had taken place locally the prior month; she claimed that "everyone" was talking about it. I mentioned that I actually had been a guest at that one, but she didn't seem to hear me: not an unusual occurrence.

A couple of Cheri's friends joined in, discussing the details of this event. All of them had comments, discussing the music, the décor and the guests, yet nobody in the conversation had been there but me. I threw in a few comments and they told me I was wrong. They explained that I didn't really know what happened that evening, but they knew because they had close friends who had been there. Attracted by the animated conversation, a couple of other women joined in. One of them started describing the event in great detail. She hadn't been there either. I gave up on that conversation.

As the evening drew on, Cheri eventually got round to telling us about her travels around the world. We were now sitting at one end of a big conference room and watching the crew at the other end, working their way through a pile of twenty-two pizzas. We were hungry, but were told to wait till the crew was done. Cheri told me that I really had to go to the French Riviera, Bali and Australia. I said that I would "take that under consideration". The crew had left the room, but we were told we couldn't have any pizza as we would mess up our clothes, and other food would be sent in later (just like "the check was in the mail"). The pizza was being saved for the cast on set.

As they were shooting the next scene, we heard they were going to dump the pizza in the garbage. We intercepted it, having decided that we were mature enough to be able to eat pizza without dropping it on our clothes.

Tempers in "background" were getting very stretched, with the extras tired and hungry. At midnight we would go into overtime, so at least that would mean higher pay rates. Of course, at 11:53 p.m. they called a wrap.

22

It's a Wrap

The show had been over for less than a month when I finished writing this book. It seemed as if it had been much longer. The show's ratings had gone down, and the remaining production schedule had been canceled. By the last two weeks, the atmosphere on the set had lost most of its energy, and had gone through anger and frustration to total disappointment. Over three hundred people had learned they would be out of a job, and even if production came back with a new show, it would probably only provide a fraction of the work that the studio had once generated.

On the other hand, from my perspective, I was very grateful that I had a chance to be part of that whole chaotic scene. As I came back into what most people would call a normal life routine, at times it felt almost as if that whole other world never existed. The show gave me an extensive "education" for more than a year. It gave me insights into a whole new aspect of my business as I learned about "production". This had always been a mystery to me, as previously I'd always worked in front of the camera, not behind it.

Not only did it give me a chance to learn new skills in production, but also the satisfaction of realizing I could take a crowd of very diverse and disorganized people and turn them into a reasonably effective working team. One time someone called me a "working class wrangler," which I took as a big compliment. When I was working, I really did work hard.

I never seriously considered quitting, even if the working conditions were unpleasant, compounded by chaos on the set. At its worst, so many things would go wrong, it was almost comical. For example, I had listened to ridiculous demands made by the stars, watched budget cuts enforced by the producers, had to pay unnecessary penalties for overtime, seen actors brought to tears, and consoled extras fired for talking on the set, for being on the phone, and even for going to the bathroom without permission . . . . and those examples were all from just one day! I would just get on with the job as we carried on shooting in dank and disorganized studio sets or locations where temperatures could range from freezing to overheated.

An obvious question was why did we all not only show up regularly, but actually scramble for jobs whenever they were offered. It certainly wasn't because of the difficult working conditions, long hours, and delayed paychecks. It was more than just thinking this could be the big break. In such a competitive business, we all felt the need to be "chosen" every day. So, no matter how difficult the last day had been, each of us wanted to be called back for the next day.

For example, it wasn't till early evening that the casting directors would get their "breakdowns": lists of what type of actors and extras they'd need for the next day. They'd then be getting calls from people both on and off the set throughout the evening, each one trying to land a better job (or any job) for the next day. For the extras and actors, it was a crazy way to try to run their lives. They might have had plans for the next day, but if they landed a job, or even an audition, then those plans went right out the door. Outside the business, not many people understood or appreciated why their "back in the real world" arrangements often got canceled at the last minute, although in my case, I always tried to warn people and get them on the phone right away to explain.

The "unemployed actor" has always been a cliché. However, in that real world outside show business, actors have always been highly employable people with skills suited to any role that called for looking people in the eye and providing a convincing story or message. I learned this as a young actress, when I was hired to work at the Boat Show in the New York Coliseum. My boss took a look at me in my stylish nautical outfit and decided to put me in the information booth. I explained that I didn't even know a bow from a stern. He just glared at me and said that I'd been hired because I was an actress and could look like I knew what I was talking about. I discovered that just projecting an image of confidence made the job easy.

So in a way, this book is a tribute to all those extras who showed persistence and ambition, even while they dealt with all the issues in their personal lives. For me, I loved the work, but once the show closed, I missed the shared experiences with the people on the set.

Since at least two-thirds of the extras I worked with were under thirty, they loved to listen to me tell stories about the "old days", mostly with sorrow in their eyes that I had to live through those terrible times before cell phones.

They enjoyed sharing their stories: some because they just liked to talk about their favorite subject (themselves), while others may have found that sharing their troubles made them feel better. A few may even have been helped by the advice or comments I gave them (at least I hope so).

In any event, I found the stories that I heard during the course of working on this show were truly amazing. I was very grateful that my colleagues were willing and able to express themselves to me in this way. As one of them said to me, "You seem like someone who cares." Over the months I had heard a lot of exaggeration and lies on this set, but I hope this comment was one of the truths: ultimately I really did care. That's why I've dedicated this book to "my" extras, who shared their life stories with me.